YOU WERE MEANT FOR ME

Single Mom By Choice

BY **SHERI STURNIOLO**

ILLUSTRATED BY

HANNAH PAK + SHAY LARBY

SECOND EDITION

"Making the decision to have a child-it is momentous.
It is to decide forever to have your heart
go walking outside your body."

- Elizabeth Stone

YouWereMeantForMeBook.com

You Were Meant For Me

Single Mom By Choice

BY **SHERI STURNIOLO**

ILLUSTRATED BY

HANNAH PAK +

SHAY LARBY

I'll tell you a story, amazing and true,
Of how you became the most wonderful you!

I could never imagine the love that would be,
When I finally knew you were meant just for me!

But first is a story that's told just before.
Before you were you.
Before you were more.

Before you were you, and not too long ago,
I was dreaming of you: I was wanting you so!
Dreams of a family and a baby to grow.
A baby to love and a baby to know.

Just like a puzzle with pieces that fit,
To make up a baby you need quite a bit!
There was love in my heart, so much love indeed,
But I knew there were other pieces I'd need.

So finding those pieces I just had to try,
To make you my baby I reached higher than high.

So out of the house, I finally flew
To ask my wise doctor: *What, oh what, could I do?*

Said the doctor to me, "You have many pieces just right.
But you'll need some more shapes so the puzzle fits tight"
"You'll be a great mother." she said with a sigh.
"So there's something amazing I know we can try"

"There are wonderful, giving people indeed,
Who happen to have just the pieces you need.
The most precious pieces made with love and with care,
These wonderful people are willing to share."

With these last, little pieces all together just so,
You became you and you started to grow!
From a dot, to a pea, to a melon you grew,
Bigger than big, 'til the day you were due.

The moment I dreamt of was soon to come true,
The moment you'd see me and I would see you.

You entered the world with a cry then a smile.
And snuggled in mommy's arms for awhile.
So precious were you: so happy were we:
Everyone shouted
with joy. "Yippie!"

The pieces they fit.
The pieces so sweet.
My dreams had come true,
The puzzle complete.

The story I tell you is truer than true,
The story of us and how you became you.

There's no doubt about it, you were meant just for me,
And forever and ever, my baby you'll be!

Questions For Your Family

Find the heart in the pile of "puzzle pieces". Why do you think this is an important "piece of the puzzle" to make up a baby? What other shapes do you see in the pile?

How does the doctor help the mommy in the book make a baby? Did a doctor help your mommy to make you?

What pieces do you see the "wonderful, giving people" holding? Are these the same pieces that the mommy was looking for to make a baby?

What piece did the "wonderful, giving people" share with your mommy so that you could grow? What pieces of the puzzle did your mommy already have?

On the day you were born, who was at the hospital to meet you for the first time?

_____

Need help answering these questions?

Visit YouWereMeantForMeBook.com

WRITE YOUR OWN STORY

Use this page to tell your child's creation story:

_____

_____

_____

_____

_____

_____

_____

_____

_____

Made in United States
North Haven, CT
19 October 2023

42889614R10015